CHARLES DICKENS

First published in 2022 by OH!
An Imprint of Welbeck Non-Fiction Limited,
part of Welbeck Publishing Group.
Based in London and Sydney.
www.welbeckpublishing.com

ISBN 978-1-80069-203-9

Compiled and written by: Stella Caldwell
Project manager: Russell Porter
Design: Stephen Cary
Production: Jess Brisley

A CIP catalogue record for this book is available from the British Library

Printed in China

10 9 8 7 6 5 4 3 2 1

THE LITTLE BOOK OF
CHARLES DICKENS

THE GREATEST STORYTELLER
OF THE VICTORIAN AGE

CONTENTS

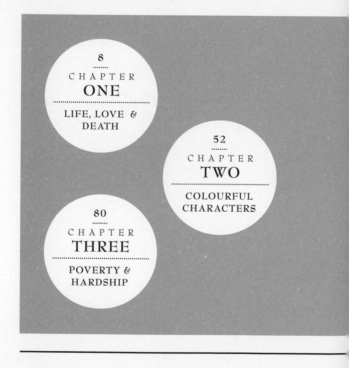

INTRODUCTION

Hailed as a literary colossus in his own lifetime, Charles Dickens is frequently regarded as the greatest novelist of the Victorian era. With 15 novels to his name, as well as novellas, short stories, travel books and essays, he was not only a brilliantly inventive storyteller, but also a superb chronicler of his age.

Dickens' literary fame began with "Boz" – the name under which he penned sharply observed sketches of Victorian society – and ended 40 years later with the cryptic, and unfinished, murder story, *The Mystery of Edwin Drood*. In works such as *Oliver Twist* or *Nicholas Nickleby*, the author combined comedy, wit and pathos to force his readers to confront the poverty, hardship and injustice that tainted the lives of the Victorian underclass.

The works of Dickens are peopled with a staggering array of unique and wonderful personalities. From the frail Little Nell of *The Old Curiosity Shop* or the pickpocketing Artful Dodger of *Oliver Twist* to the decaying spinster, Miss Havisham, of *Great Expectations* or the vengeful Madame Defarge in *A Tale of Two Cities*, his characters are some of the most memorable in English Literature. A few of them, such as the miserly Scrooge in *A Christmas Carol*, have even become defining terms in everyday vernacular.

It is fascinating to see how Dickens' own colourful life helped to shape his fiction. His first-hand experience of poverty and childhood labour influenced works such as *Little Dorrit* and the autobiographical *David Copperfield*, while the legal knowledge he gained as a young clerk and parliamentary journalist proved indispensable for works such as *The Pickwick Papers* or *Bleak House*.

More than 200 years after his birth, Dickens' name is respected and revered around the world while his books have never been out of print. Showcasing fabulous quotes from his writings – by turns, witty, comic, insightful and wise – alongside fascinating facts about his life and achievements, this delightful volume is a fitting tribute to a literary giant.

....

CHAPTER
ONE

LIFE, LOVE & DEATH

Dickens was the great novelist of his age, representing its manners, virtues and vices. He saw the business of living in all its shades: the high comedy, the tragic pathos, and much in between. Always entertaining, Dickens' works also reveal a profound understanding of human nature.

"A wonderful fact to reflect upon, that every human creature is constituted to be that profound secret and mystery to every other. A solemn consideration, when I enter a great city by night, that every one of those darkly clustered houses encloses its own secret; that every room in every one of them encloses its own secret…

...that every beating heart in the hundreds of thousands of breasts there, is, in some of its imaginings, a secret to the heart nearest it! Something of the awfulness, even of Death itself, is referable to this."

A Tale of Two Cities, 1859

Charles Dickens, the second of eight children, was born on 7 February 1812, in Portsmouth, England. His father, John, worked as a clerk in the Navy Pay Office.

In 1814, John moved his family to London, and then, two years later, to Chatham, Kent. This was the place where Dickens spent the happiest years of his childhood, until financial difficulties brought the family back to London in 1822.

"**P**ause you who read this, and think for a moment of the long chain of iron or gold, of thorns or flowers, that would never have bound you, but for the formation of the first link on one memorable day."

Great Expectations, 1861

"If there be any who have never known the blank that follows death – the weary void – the sense of desolation that will come upon the strongest minds, when something familiar and beloved is missed at every turn – the connection between inanimate and senseless things, and the object of recollection, when every household god becomes a monument and every room a grave...

…If there be any who have not known this, and proved it by their own experience, they can never faintly guess how, for many days, the old man pined and moped away the time, and wandered here and there as seeking something, and had no comfort."

The Old Curiosity Shop, 1841

"I loved you madly; in the distasteful work of the day, in the wakeful misery of the night, girded by sordid realities, or wandering through Paradises and Hells of visions into which I rushed, carrying your image in my arms, I loved you madly."

The Mystery of Edwin Drood, 1870

"You know what I am going to say. I love you. What other men may mean when they use that expression, I cannot tell; what I mean is, that I am under the influence of some tremendous attraction which I have resisted in vain, and which overmasters me."

Our Mutual Friend, 1865

"There is something about a roused woman: especially if she add to all her other strong passions, the fierce impulses of recklessness and despair; which few men like to provoke."

Oliver Twist, 1839

"Love her, love her, love her! If she favours you, love her. If she wounds you, love her. If she tears your heart to pieces — and as it gets older and stronger, it will tear deeper — love her, love her, love her!"

Great Expectations, 1861

Illustration by F.O.C Darley, from an 1863 edition of *Hard Times*

"It is said that every life has its roses and thorns; there seemed, however, to have been a misadventure or mistake in Stephen's case, whereby somebody else had become possessed of his roses, and he had become possessed of somebody else's thorns in addition to his own."

Hard Times, 1854

"Now, when suffering has been stronger than all other teaching, and has taught me to understand what your heart used to be. I have been bent and broken, but — I hope — into a better shape."

Great Expectations, 1861

"For, Evil often stops short at itself and dies with the doer of it; but Good, never."

Our Mutual Friend, 1865

In 1824, an unpaid debt landed Dickens' father in Marshalsea debtors' prison – later the setting of *Little Dorrit*. Dickens' mother and siblings were also imprisoned while Dickens was sent to work at Warren's Blacking Factory, sticking labels on jars of shoe polish and living alone in lodgings.

This traumatic experience, at the age of just 12, scarred him permanently – but would also inspire some of his finest writing.

"Thirty years ago there stood, a few doors short of the church of Saint George, in the borough of Southwark, on the left-hand side of the way going southward, the Marshalsea Prison. It had stood there many years before, and it remained there some years afterwards; but it is gone now, and the world is none the worse without it."

Dickens introduces Marshalsea debtor's prison,
Little Dorrit, 1857

"Hope to the last!" said Newman, clapping him on the back. "Always hope; that's dear boy. Never leave off hoping; it don't answer. Do you mind me, Nick? it don't answer. Don't leave a stone unturned. It's always something, to know you've done the most you could. But, don't leave off hoping, or it's of no use doing anything. Hope, hope, to the last!"

Nicholas Nickleby, 1839

"I confess I have yet to learn
that a lesson of the purest good
may not be drawn from
the vilest evil."

Oliver Twist, 1839

"**D**ignity, and even holiness too, sometimes, are more questions of coat and waistcoat than some people imagine."

Oliver Twist, 1839

"**M**oths, and all sorts of ugly creatures ... hover about a lighted candle. Can the candle help it?"

Great Expectations, 1861

Illustration by Phiz (Hablot K. Browne), from the original edition of *David Copperfield*

"I know enough of the world now, to have almost lost the capacity of being much surprised by anything.**"**

David Copperfield, 1850

"When a man bleeds inwardly, it is a dangerous thing for himself; but when he laughs inwardly, it bodes no good to other people."

The Pickwick Papers, 1837

"He looked like death; not death as it shows in shroud and coffin, but in the guise it wears when life has just departed; when a young and gentle spirit has, but an instant, fled to Heaven, and the gross air of the world has not had time to breathe upon the changing dust it hallowed."

Oliver Twist, 1839

At the age of 15, Dickens found
work as a junior clerk in a law office
— the knowledge he gleaned here
about the judicial system would
work itself into novels such as *The
Pickwick Papers* and *Bleak House*.

Dickens also learned the shorthand
method of writing developed by
Thomas Gurney, a skill that allowed
him to find work as a parliamentary
journalist in the 1830s.

"I the reputation behind me of being the best and most rapid Reporter ever known ... I could do anything in that way under any sort of circumstances – and often did."

Letter to his friend Wilkie Collins,
describing his time as a reporter, 6 June 1856

"The broken heart. You think you will die, but you just keep living, day after day after terrible day."

Great Expectations, 1861

"The pain of parting is nothing to the joy of meeting again."

Nicholas Nickleby, 1839

"**O**ut of my thoughts! You are part of my existence, part of myself. You have been in every line I have ever read, since I first came here … You have been in every prospect I have ever seen since … in the clouds, in the light, in the darkness, in the wind, in the woods, in the sea, in the streets."

Great Expectations, 1861

"**B**ah," said Scrooge, "Humbug."

A Christmas Carol, 1843

"I looked at the stars, and considered how awful it would be for a man to turn his face up to them as he froze to death, and see no help or pity in all the glittering multitude."

Great Expectations, 1861

"What a fine thing capital punishment is! Dead men never repent; dead men never bring awkward stories to light. The prospect of the gallows, too, makes them hardy and bold. Ah, it's a fine thing for the trade! Five of them strung up in a row, and none left to play booty or turn white-livered!"

Oliver Twist, 1839

"Love, though said to be afflicted with blindness, is a vigilant watchman."

Our Mutual Friend, 1865

"It is a far, far better thing that I do, than I have ever done; it is a far, far better rest that I go to than I have ever known."

A Tale of Two Cities, 1859

"And O there are days in this life, worth life and worth death. And O what a bright old song it is, that O 'tis love, 'tis love, 'tis love that makes the world go round!"

Our Mutual Friend, 1865

" He was bolder in the daylight
— most men are. "

The Pickwick Papers, 1837

"Constancy in love is a good thing; but it means nothing, and is nothing, without constancy in every kind of effort."

Bleak House, 1853

"No space of regret can make amends for one life's opportunity misused."

A Christmas Carol, 1843

Dickens' first literary effort, a sketch called "A Dinner at Poplar Walk", was published in 1833. Further sketches, offering delightful glimpses of life in early Victorian London, soon followed.

Looking for a memorable pen name, Dickens settled on "Boz" – it came from the way in which his younger brother Augustus pronounced his own nickname Moses, as "Boses". In 1936, the pieces were published in book form as *Sketches by Boz*.

"Mr Augustus Minns was a bachelor, of about forty as he said — of about eight-and-forty as his friends said. He was always exceedingly clean, precise, and tidy: perhaps somewhat priggish, and the most retiring man in the world."

The first lines of Dickens' first published story, originally titled "A Dinner at Poplar Walk" (1833), and later titled "Mr Minns and his Cousin"

"Death may beget life, but oppression can beget nothing other than itself."

A Tale of Two Cities, 1859

"He went to church, and walked about the streets, and watched the people hurrying to and fro, and patted children on the head, and questioned beggars, and looked down into the kitchens of houses, and up to the windows, and found that everything could yield him pleasure. He had never dreamed that any walk – that anything – could give him so much happiness."

A Christmas Carol, 1843

CHAPTER
TWO

COLOURFUL CHARACTERS

No other novelist has created so many characters that people still recognize today: The Artful Dodger, Little Nell, Scrooge, Miss Havisham – the list goes on. Villainous, angelic, rambunctious or heartbreaking, these larger-than-life personalities are magnificently unforgettable.

"The wine was so bitter cold
that it forced a little scream from
Miss Tox … The veal had come
from such an airy pantry, that
the first taste of it had struck
a sensation as of cold lead to Mr
Chick's extremities. Mr Dombey
alone remained unmoved. He
might have been hung up for sale
at a Russian fair as a specimen
of a frozen gentleman."

Dombey and Son, 1848

"He ate hard eggs, shell and all, devoured gigantic prawns with the heads and tails on, chewed tobacco and water-cresses at the same time and with extraordinary greediness, drank boiling tea without winking."

Description of Daniel Quilp,
The Old Curiosity Shop, 1841

"Oh! But he was a tight-fisted hand at the grind-stone, Scrooge! a squeezing, wrenching, grasping, scraping, clutching, covetous, old sinner! Hard and sharp as flint, from which no steel had ever struck out generous fire; secret, and self-contained, and solitary as an oyster."

Description of Ebenezer Scrooge,
A Christmas Carol, 1843

Illustration by John Leech, from the original edition of *A Christmas Carol*

In 1830, Dickens fell deeply in love with Maria Beadnell. Her wealthy parents felt Dickens lacked prospects, however, and the relationship came to an end in early 1833.

Twenty-four years later, Maria contacted the now-famous author and they agreed to meet. Dickens was disillusioned to find that Maria's charms and looks had faded. He later based the character of Flora Finching, in *Little Dorrit*, on his former sweetheart.

"Flora, always tall, had grown to be very broad too, and short of breath … Flora, whom he had left a lily, had become a peony; but that was not much. Flora, who had seemed enchanting … was diffuse and silly. That was much. Flora, who had been spoiled and artless long ago, was determined to be spoiled and artless now. That was a fatal blow."

Description of Flora Finching, the former sweetheart of Arthur Clennam, *Little Dorrit*, 1857

"**M**r Bucket notices things in general, with a face as unchanging as the great mourning ring on his little finger or the brooch, composed of not much diamond and a good deal of setting, which he wears in his shirt."

Description of Inspector Bucket,
Bleak House, 1853

"Opening her arms wide, [she] took my curly head within them, and gave it a good squeeze. I know it was a good squeeze, because, being very plump, whenever she made any little exertion after she was dressed, some of the buttons on the back of her gown flew off. And I recollect two bursting to the opposite side of the parlour."

Description of David Copperfield's nurse, Clara Peggotty, *David Copperfield*, 1850

At the age of 24, Dickens married the daughter of his editor, Catherine Hogarth. Over the next 15 years, the couple had 10 children , seven boys and three girls.

Dickens often expressed frustration at what he saw as his children's lack of ambition or focus. He once lamented that he had "brought up the largest family ever known, with the smallest disposition to do anything for themselves".

"He encouraged us in every possible way to make ourselves useful, and … to be ever tidy and neat … [He] made a point of visiting every room in the house once each morning, and if a chair was out of its place, or a blind not quite straight, or a crumb left on the floor, woe betide the offender."

Dickens' daughter Mamie recalls her father,
in her memoir published after his death

"A fearful man, all in coarse grey, with a great iron on his leg … A man who had been soaked in water, and smothered in mud … and stung by nettles, and torn by briars; who limped, and shivered, and glared and growled; and whose teeth chattered in his head as he seized me by the chin."

Pip meets Abel Magwitch, *Great Expectations*, 1861

"**I** found Uriah reading a great fat book, with such demonstrative attention, that his lank forefinger followed up every line as he read, and made clammy tracks along the page (or so I fully believed) like a snail."

Description of Uriah Heep, whose name
has become a byword for a falsely humble hypocrite,
David Copperfield, 1850

Illustration by Phiz (Hablot K. Browne), from the original edition of *The Pickwick Papers*

"**O**ut vith it, as the father said to his child, when he swallowed a farden."

A linguistic pearl – or "wellerism" as such sayings have come to be known – from the Cockney shoe shiner Sam Weller, *The Pickwick Papers*, 1837

"He wore a man's coat, which reached nearly to his heels. He had turned the cuffs back, half-way up his arm, to get his hands out of the sleeves … He was, altogether, as roystering and swaggering a young gentleman as ever stood four feet six, or something less, in his bluchers."

Description of Jack Dawkins, or The Artful Dodger,
Oliver Twist, 1839

"He wore the aspect of a man who was always lying in wait for something that WOULDN'T come to pass."

Description of the treacherous Mr Gashford,
Barnaby Rudge, 1841

"Madame Defarge knitted with nimble fingers and steady eyebrows, and saw nothing."

Dickens introduces the vengeful
Madame Defarge,
A Tale of Two Cities, 1859

Illustration by Fred Barnard, from an 1874
edition of *A Tale of Two Cities*

WHAT'S IN A NAME?

Dickens is famous for the unforgettable names he bestowed upon his characters. Here are eight of the best:

Serjeant Buzfuz – *The Pickwick Papers*

Uriah Heep – *David Copperfield*

Uncle Pumblechook – *Great Expectations*

Hiram Grewgious – *The Mystery of Edwin Drood*

Simon Tappertit – *Barnaby Rudge*

Ebenezer Scrooge – *A Christmas Carol*

Affery Flintwinch – *Little Dorrit*

Bayham Badger – *Bleak House*

"I had heard of Miss Havisham up town – everybody for miles around, had heard of Miss Havisham up town – as an immensely rich and grim old lady who lived in a large and dismal house barricaded against robbers, and who led a life of seclusion."

Pip recounts what he knows of the reclusive
Miss Havisham, *Great Expectations*, 1861

The emphasis was helped by the speaker's mouth, which was wide, thin, and hard set … The speaker's obstinate carriage, square coat, square legs, square shoulders – nay, his very neckcloth, trained to take him by the throat with an unaccommodating grasp, like a stubborn fact, as it was – all helped the emphasis.

Description of Tom Gradgrind, *Hard Times*, 1854

"What have paupers to do with soul or spirit? It's quite enough that we let 'em have live bodies. If you had kept the boy on gruel, ma'am, this would never have happened."

Mr Bumble, the beadle of the poor workhouse, shows his cruelty, *Oliver Twist*, 1839

"She was dead. No sleep so beautiful and calm, so free from trace of pain, so fair to look upon. She seemed a creature fresh from the hand of God, and waiting for the breath of life; not one who has lived and suffered death. Dear, gentle, patient, noble Nell was dead."

The death of Little Nell,
The Old Curiosity Shop, 1841

"Some people likened him to a direction-post, which is always telling the way to a place, and never goes there.**"**

Dickens evokes the hypocrisy of Seth Pecksniff,
Martin Chuzzlewit, 1844

The Posthumous Papers of the Pickwick Club was published in monthly parts from April 1836. A sensational success, it was published in book form in 1837.

Dickens now embarked on a full-time career as a novelist, producing work at an incredible rate.

Almost all his books were published first in weekly or monthly installments, popularizing the idea of the "cliff-hanger" ending.

"Mr Pickwick ... took a survey of the man of business, who was an elderly, pimply-faced, vegetable-diet sort of man, in a black coat, dark mixture trousers, and small black gaiters; a kind of being who seemed to be an essential part of the desk at which he was writing, and to have as much thought or sentiment."

The Pickwick Papers, 1837

CHAPTER
THREE

POVERTY &
HARDSHIP

A social realist, Dickens used
his novels to make scathing
criticisms of Victorian England.
Moving from the refined
drawing rooms of the upper
classes to the horrors of the
poor workhouse, his writing
highlighted the grinding poverty
and deprivation that was the lot
of all too many.

"To be shelterless and alone in the open country ... to listen to the falling rain, and crouch for warmth beneath the lee of some old barn or rick, or in the hollow of a tree; are dismal things – but not so dismal as the wandering up and down where shelter is, and beds and sleepers are by thousands; a houseless rejected creature."

Barnaby Rudge, 1841

"This is the even-handed dealing of the world!" he said. "There is nothing on which it is so hard as poverty; and there is nothing it professes to condemn with such severity as the pursuit of wealth!"

A Christmas Carol, 1843

"It was a town of red brick, or of brick that would have been red if the smoke and ashes had allowed it; but as matters stood, it was a town of unnatural red and black like the painted face of a savage. It was a town of machinery and tall chimneys, out of which interminable serpents of smoke trailed themselves for ever and ever, and never got uncoiled."

Hard Times, 1854

"It is said that the children of the very poor are not brought up, but dragged up.**"**

Bleak House, 1853

Dickens' second novel, *Oliver Twist*, came as a shock to his readers, who were expecting more comedy in the vein of *The Pickwick Papers*.

The author used the hard-hitting story to draw attention to social ills, describing child neglect in orphanages, inhuman conditions in the poor workhouses, crime and prostitution.

"Bleak, dark, and piercing cold, it was a night for the well-housed and fed to draw round the bright fire, and thank God they were at home; and for the homeless starving wretch to lay him down and die. Many hunger-worn outcasts close their eyes in our bare streets at such times, who, let their crimes have been what they may, can hardly open them in a more bitter world."

Oliver Twist, 1839

"The [board members] were very sage, deep, philosophical men; and when they came to turn their attention to the workhouse ... they established the rule that all poor people should have the alternative (for they would compel nobody, not they) of being starved by a gradual process in the house, or by a quick one out of it...

…With this view, they contracted with the waterworks to lay on an unlimited supply of water, and with a corn-factor to supply periodically small quantities of oatmeal, and issued three meals of thin gruel a day, with an onion twice a week and half a roll on Sundays."

Oliver Twist, 1839

"Please, sir, I want some more."

Oliver Twist, 1839

Illustration by James Mahoney, for an 1871
edition of *Oliver Twist*

"It is a dreadful thing to wait and watch for the approach of death; to know that hope is gone, and recovery impossible; and to sit and count the dreary hours through long, long, nights — such nights as only watchers by the bed of sickness know."

"The Drunkard's Death", *Sketches by Boz*, 1836

"Annual income twenty pounds, annual expenditure nineteen nineteen six, result happiness. Annual income twenty pounds, annual expenditure twenty pounds ought and six, result misery."

David Copperfield, 1850

FLAIR FOR WORDS

More than 200 words and compounds
in the *Oxford English Dictionary* are cited
as having been first used by Dickens.
Here are just a few examples:

Devil-May-Care *(The Pickwick Papers)*

The Creeps *(David Copperfield)*

Round the Clock *(Bleak House)*

Dustbin *(Dombey and Son)*

Slow-coach *(The Pickwick Papers)*

Abuzz *(A Tale of Two Cities)*

"**V**irtue shows quite as well in rags and patches as she does in purple and fine linen."

Speech at a dinner held in his honour in Boston, US, 1 February 1842

"Dead, your Majesty. Dead, my lords and gentlemen. Dead, right reverends and wrong reverends of every order. Dead, men and women, born with heavenly compassion in your hearts. And dying thus around us every day."

Bleak House, 1853

"Pale and haggard faces, lank and bony figures, children with the countenances of old men ... there were the bleared eye, the hare-lip, the crooked foot, and every ugliness or distortion that told of unnatural aversion conceived by parents for their offspring, or of young lives which ... had been one horrible endurance of cruelty and neglect."

Nicholas Nickleby, 1839

"Fog everywhere … Fog in the eyes and throats of ancient Greenwich pensioners, wheezing by the firesides of their wards; fog in the stem and bowl of the afternoon pipe of the wrathful skipper … fog cruelly pinching the toes and fingers of his shivering little prentice boy on deck."

Bleak House, 1853

"If they would rather die," said Scrooge, "they had better do it, and decrease the surplus population."

A Christmas Carol, 1843

Dickens spent more than a decade working on a project to help what he described as "fallen" young women. Supported by the banking heiress Angela Burdett-Coutts, he established a safe house in Shepherd's Bush, called Urania Cottage.

The aim was to provide an environment where women could rise out of lives of prostitution and crime by learning skills that would help them to find useful employment.

"In this home, which stands in a pleasant country lane and where each may have her little flower-garden if she pleases, they will be treated with the greatest kindness: will lead an active, cheerful, healthy life: will learn many things it is profitable and good to know, and … will begin life afresh and be able to win a good name and character."

Dickens' pamphlet *An Appeal To Fallen Women*, 1849

"To pace the echoing stones from hour to hour, counting the dull chimes of the clocks; to watch the lights twinkling in chamber windows, to think what happy forgetfulness each house shuts in ... to feel, by the wretched contrast with everything on every hand, more utterly alone and cast away than in a trackless desert..."

Barnaby Rudge, 1841

"Bob said he didn't believe there ever was such a goose cooked … Eked out by apple-sauce and mashed potatoes, it was a sufficient dinner for the whole family; indeed, as Mrs Cratchit said with great delight (surveying one small atom of a bone upon the dish), they hadn't ate it all at last!"

A Christmas Carol, 1843

Dickens kept at least three pet ravens during his lifetime, all of them called "Grip".

When the original Grip died of lead poisoning – after eating paint scraped from furniture – Dickens had him stuffed and mounted in a case, which he kept above his writing desk.

Grip appears as a character in Dickens' fifth novel, *Barnaby Rudge*.

"The raven in this story is a compound of two great originals, of whom I was, at different times, the proud possessor."

Illustration by Phiz (Hablot K. Browne), for the
original edition of *Barnaby Rudge*

Preface to *Barnaby Rudge*, 1841

"Gin-drinking is a great vice in England, but wretchedness and dirt are a greater; and until you improve the homes of the poor, or persuade a half-famished wretch not to seek relief in the temporary oblivion of his own misery … gin-shops will increase in number and splendour."

"Gin Shops", *Sketches by Boz*, 1936

"Where graceful youth should have filled their features out, and touched them with its freshest tints, a stale and shrivelled hand, like that of age, had pinched, and twisted them, and pulled them into shreds. Where angels might have sat enthroned, devils lurked, and glared out menacing."

A Christmas Carol, 1843

CHAPTER
FOUR

LAUGHTER & GOOD HUMOUR

The runaway success of *The Pickwick Papers* announced Dickens' flair for comedy. The 1830s and '40s were full of comic writers, but Dickens, with his talent for satire, word play and creating larger-than-life characters, made his readers laugh as no other writer had ever done.

"It is a fair, even-handed, noble adjustment of things, that while there is infection in disease and sorrow, there is nothing in the world so irresistibly contagious as laughter and good-humour."

A Christmas Carol, 1843

"In the majority of cases, conscience is an elastic and very flexible article."

The Old Curiosity Shop, 1841

Fascinated by the paranormal, Dickens had what his friend and biographer John Foster called "a hankering after ghosts". Along with authors such as Arthur Conan Doyle and William Butler Yeats, he was a member of "The Ghost Club", which attempted to investigate hauntings.

He was also interested in mesmerism, the practice of putting people into hypnotic trances to cure illnesses and disease.

"As the gloom and shadow thickened behind him, in that place where it had been gathering so darkly, it took, by slow degrees … an awful likeness of himself! Ghastly and cold, colourless in its leaden face and hands, but with his features, and his bright eyes, and his grizzled hair, and dressed in the gloomy shadow of his dress…"

The Haunted Man and the Ghost's Bargain, 1848

"Any man may be in good spirits and good temper when he's well dressed. There ain't much credit in that."

Martin Chuzzlewit, 1844

PROLIFIC WRITER

Dickens wrote 15 novels as well as novellas (such as the hugely popular *A Christmas Carol*), short stories and essays. Here are a few novel facts:

First: *The Pickwick Papers*

Longest (by word count): *David Copperfield*

Shortest (complete novel): *Hard Times*

Last: *The Mystery of Edwin Drood*

Bestselling: *A Tale of Two Cities*

Funniest: *The Pickwick Papers*

Most romantic: *Great Expectations*

Dickens' personal favourite:
David Copperfield

"Dumb as a drum vith a hole in it, Sir."

The Pickwick Papers, 1837

"**M**r Parkes, finding himself in the position of having got into metaphysics without exactly seeing his way out of them, stammered forth an apology and retreated from the argument."

Barnaby Rudge, 1841

Illustration by Phiz (Hablot K. Browne), from the original edition of *Bleak House*

"There were two classes of charitable people: one, the people who did a little and made a great deal of noise; the other, the people who did a great deal and made no noise at all."

Bleak House, 1853

"Dombey sat in the corner of the darkened room in the great arm-chair by the bedside, and Son lay tucked up warm in a little basket bedstead, carefully disposed on a low settee immediately in front of the fire and close to it, as if his constitution were analogous to that of a muffin, and it was essential to toast him brown while he was very new."

Dombey and Son, 1848

Dickens contributed to and edited
journals throughout his writing career.
In 1850, he co-founded *Household
Words*, a weekly magazine that ran
for a decade. Costing a tuppence and
edited entirely by Dickens, it featured
colourful news features, short stories,
poetry and essays.

All Year Round, founded by Dickens
in 1860, was similar to its predecessor,
but also published serial fiction,
such as Dickens' own novel *A Tale
of Two Cities*.

"But, tears were not the things to find their way to Mr Bumble's soul; his heart was waterproof."

Oliver Twist, 1839

"I have made up my mind that I must have money, Pa. I feel that I can't beg it, borrow it, or steal it; and so I have resolved that I must marry it."

Our Mutual Friend, 1865

"A modest ring at the bell at length allayed her fears, and Miss Benton, hurrying into her own room and shutting herself up, in order that she might preserve that appearance of being taken by surprise which is so essential to the polite reception of visitors, awaited their coming with a smiling countenance."

Master Humphry's Clock, 1840

A natural performer, Dickens had
originally wanted to be an actor.

From 1842, he and his friend
John Foster worked on a series of high-
quality amateur productions,
with Dickens himself dazzling in
several roles.

Later, Dickens used his acting skills to
give electrifying readings from
his novels across Britain and in the US.
These reading tours were a sensational
success and earned Dickens a great
deal of money.

"It was as true ... as turnips is. It was as true ... as taxes is. And nothing's truer than them."

David Copperfield, 1850

"Peggotty!" repeated Miss Betsey, with some indignation. "Do you mean to say, child, that any human being has gone into a Christian church, and got herself named Peggotty?"

David Copperfield, 1850

" It being a part of Mrs Pipchin's
system not to encourage a child's
mind to develop and expand
itself like a young flower, but to
open it by force like an oyster. "

Dombey and Son, 1848

Illustration by Phiz (Hablot K. Browne), from the original edition of *Dombey and Son*

"**M**ATRIMONY is proverbially a serious undertaking. Like an overweening predilection for brandy-and-water, it is a misfortune into which a man easily falls, and from which he finds it remarkably difficult to extricate himself."

"A Passage in the Life of Mr Watkins Tottle",
Sketches by Boz, 1835

"Mr and Mrs Boffin sat staring at mid-air, and Mrs Wilfer sat silently giving them to understand that every breath she drew required to be drawn with a self-denial rarely paralleled in history."

Our Mutual Friend, 1865

Dickens was at the height of his fame when he first travelled to the US, in 1842. Followed everywhere by adoring fans, he came to hate the attention and later wrote scathingly about the country and its people.

Dickens returned to the US in 1867, this time to do a reading tour. Although his health was now in decline, the tour was a sell-out success, and a conciliatory Dickens made s ome amends for his previous negative comments.

"There are very few moments in a man's existence when he experiences so much ludicrous distress, or meets with so little charitable commiseration, as when he is in pursuit of his own hat."

The Pickwick Papers, 1837

"Poetry's unnat'ral; no man ever talked poetry 'cept a beadle on boxin' day, or Warren's blackin' or Rowland's oil, or some o' them low fellows; never you let yourself down to talk poetry, my boy."

The Pickwick Papers, 1837

"Mr Bazzard's father, being a Norfolk farmer, would have furiously laid about him with a flail, a pitch-fork, and every agricultural implement available for assaulting purposes, on the slightest hint of his son's having written a play."

The Mystery of Edwin Drood, 1870

"There is no such passion
in human nature, as the passion
for gravy among commercial
gentlemen."

Martin Chuzzlewit, 1844

"**H**e appeared to enjoy beyond everything the sound of his own voice. I couldn't wonder at that, for it was mellow and full and gave great importance to every word he uttered. He listened to himself with obvious satisfaction and sometimes gently beat time to his own music with his head or rounded a sentence with his hand."

Bleak House, 1853

Dickens wrote his runaway bestseller *A Christmas Carol* in just six weeks.

Published on 19 December 1843, the novella had sold out by Christmas Eve. By the close of 1844, it had already gone through 13 printings.

The book helped to revive the celebration of Christmas, and Dickens' name has been synonymous with the season ever since.

"In half a minute Mrs Cratchit entered – flushed, but smiling proudly – with the pudding, like a speckled cannon-ball, so hard and firm, blazing in half of half-a-quartern of ignited brandy, and bedight with Christmas holly stuck into the top."

A Christmas Carol, 1843

CHAPTER
FIVE

OBSERVATIONS

Celebrated for his extraordinary
powers of observation, Dickens
conjured up a colourful view of
19th-century society. His ability to
set a scene, immersing the reader in
time and place, gave rise to richly
evocative passages.

"It was the best of times, it was the worst of times, it was the age of wisdom, it was the age of foolishness, it was the epoch of belief, it was the epoch of incredulity, it was the season of Light, it was the season of Darkness, it was the spring of hope, it was the winter of despair…"

A Tale of Two Cities, 1859

"As he glided stealthily along, creeping beneath the shelter of the walls and doorways, the hideous old man seemed like some loathsome reptile, engendered in the slime and darkness through which he moved: crawling forth, by night, in search of some rich offal for a meal."

Oliver Twist, 1839

"I informed Mr Micawber that I relied upon him for a bowl of punch … His recent despondency, not to say despair, was gone in a moment. I never saw a man so thoroughly enjoy himself amid the fragrance of lemon-peel and sugar, the odour of burning rum … as Mr Micawber did that afternoon."

David Copperfield, 1850

"The sky was dark and gloomy, the air was damp and raw, the streets were wet and sloppy. The smoke hung sluggishly above the chimney-tops as if it lacked the courage to rise, and the rain came slowly and doggedly down, as if it had not even the spirit to pour."

The Pickwick Papers, 1837

Dickens' eighth novel, *David Copperfield*, is written with a first-person narrator and contains many autobiographical elements.

Creakle, the school headmaster in the novel, resembles the headmaster in Dickens' school.

David's experiences of child labour reflect Dickens' own traumatic experience, and Mr Micawber, imprisoned for debt, is like Dickens' own father.

"Like many fond parents,
I have in my heart of hearts a
favourite child. And his name is
David Copperfield."

Dickens' preface to *David Copperfield,* 1850

"Ah! People need to rise early, to see the sun in all his splendour, for his brightness seldom lasts the day through. The morning of day and the morning of life are but too much alike."

The Pickwick Papers, 1837

"Charles Darnay seemed to stand in a company of the dead. Ghosts all! The ghost of beauty, the ghost of stateliness, the ghost of elegance, the ghost of pride, the ghost of frivolity, the ghost of wit, the ghost of youth, the ghost of age, all waiting their dismissal from the desolate shore…"

A Tale of Two Cities, 1859

"I don't mean to say that I know … what there is particularly dead about a door-nail. I might have been inclined, myself, to regard a coffin-nail as the deadest piece of ironmongery in the trade. But the wisdom of our ancestors is in the simile … You will therefore permit me to repeat, emphatically, that Marley was as dead as a door-nail."

A Christmas Carol, 1843

"My father had left a small collection of books in a little room upstairs … From that blessed little room, Roderick Random, Peregrine Pickle, Humphrey Clinker, Tom Jones, the Vicar of Wakefield, Don Quixote, Gil Blas, and Robinson Crusoe, came out, a glorious host, to keep me company."

David Copperfield, 1850

At the age of 45, Dickens became infatuated with an 18-year-old actress called Ellen Ternan. Letters show that he had grown increasingly dissatisfied with his wife, Catherine, and within a year the pair had separated.

Catherine moved out of the family homes and Dickens cut off contact between her and her younger children. As rumours about Dickens' love life swirled, he attempted to calm the situation by publishing a letter in the *Times*.

"I believe my marriage has been for years and years as miserable a one as ever was made … I believe that no two people were ever created with such an impossibility of interest, sympathy, confidence, sentiment, tender union of any kind between them as there is between my wife and me."

Letter to Angela Burdett Couts,
9 May 1858

"The most prominent object was a long table ... as if a feast had been in preparation when the house and the clocks all stopped together. An epergne or centerpiece ... was heavily overhung with cobwebs ... and, as I looked along the yellow expanse ... I saw speckled-legged spiders with blotchy bodies running home to it, and running out from it."

Description of Miss Havisham's wedding breakfast,
Great Expectations, 1861

Illustration by John McLenan, from the American edition (1861) of *Great Expectations*

As Ellen Ternan – or "Nelly" –
took on more importance in Dickens'
life, he moved her into a
London townhouse bought in her
sisters' names.

Determined to protect his reputation,
Dickens went to great lengths to
cover up their relationship. Nelly
gave up acting and remained largely
isolated – apart from her close
relationships with her mother and
sisters – until Dickens' death.

"If I may so express it, I was steeped in Dora. I was not merely over head and ears in love with her, but I was saturated through and through."

David Copperfield, 1850

"The rooks were sailing about the cathedral towers; and the towers themselves … were cutting the bright morning air, as if there were no such thing as change on earth. Yet the bells, when they sounded, told me sorrowfully of … their own age, and my pretty Dora's youth; and of the many, never old, who had lived and loved and died."

David Copperfield, 1850

"The sun – the bright sun, that brings back, not light alone, but new life, and hope, and freshness to man – burst upon the crowded city in clear and radiant glory. Through costly-coloured glass and paper-mended window, through cathedral dome and rotten crevice, it shed its equal ray."

Oliver Twist, 1839

"Melancholy streets, in a penitential garb of soot, steeped the souls of the people who were condemned to look at them out of windows, in dire despondency. In every thoroughfare, up almost every alley, and down almost every turning, some doleful bell was throbbing, jerking, tolling, as if the Plague were in the city and the dead-carts were going round."

Little Dorrit, 1857

Illustration by Phiz (Hablot K. Browne), from the original edition of *Little Dorrit*

In June 1865, Dickens had a close brush with death. Accompanied by his mistress, Ellen Ternan, and her mother, he was on a train from Folkestone to London when it crashed in Staplehurst, Kent.

After helping the Ternans to escape, Dickens tended to the injured and dying, an experience that would profoundly affect him. Ten of the 100 passengers were killed and many more were seriously hurt.

"I remember with devout thankfulness that I can never be much nearer parting company with my readers for ever than I was then, until there shall be written against my life, the two words with which I have this day closed this book: – THE END."

The postscript to *Our Mutual Friend*,
the book Dickens was writing when he was involved in
the Staplehurst disaster

CHAPTER
SIX

WISE WORDS

Dickens' works are peppered
with quick wit, clever insights
and sparkling bon mots.
More than 150 years after his
death, many of his phrases are
instantly recognizable while
much of his advice seems as
relevant as it ever did.

"**I** will honour Christmas in my heart, and try to keep it all the year."

A Christmas Carol, 1843

"Trifles make the sum of life."

David Copperfield, 1850

" Change begets change.
Nothing propagates so fast. "

Martin Chuzzlewit, 1844

WISE WORDS

Illustration by Phiz (Hablot K. Browne), from the original edition of *Martin Chuzzlewit*

LONDON LOCATIONS

Dickens routinely walked London's streets, taking in the sights, sounds and smells of the old city. Here are five locations associated with the author:

48 DOUGHTY STREET (WC1N 2LX) – The home where Dickens penned his first three novels, now The Charles Dickens Museum.

THE OLD CURIOSITY SHOP (13-14 Portsmouth Street, WC2A 2ES) – This 16th-century building was the inspiration for Dickens' novel of the same name.

THE GEORGE AND VULTURE
(3 Castle Court, EC3V 9DL)
Mentioned no less than 20 times in
The Pickwick Papers, this historic pub was
a favourite drinking haunt of Dickens.

THE SEVEN DIALS
This area of Covent Garden, in central
London, was a notorious slum in
Dickens' day. He roamed its filthy,
vice-ridden alleys, writing portraits that
made up *Sketches by Boz*.

LONDON BRIDGE
(SE1 9BG) – Dickens loved to look at the
view from this bridge, one of the most
mentioned locations in his novels.

"My meaning simply is, that whatever I have tried to do in life, I have tried with all my heart to do well; that whatever I have devoted myself to, I have devoted myself to completely; that in great aims and in small, I have always been thoroughly in earnest."

David Copperfield, 1850

"The most important thing in life is to stop saying 'I wish' and start saying 'I will'. Consider nothing impossible, then treat possibilities as probabilities."

David Copperfield, 1850

"To remember happiness which cannot be restored, is pain, but of a softened kind."

Nicholas Nickleby, 1839

"Take nothing on its looks; take everything on evidence. There's no better rule."

Great Expectations, 1861

Dickens had a secret door installed in his study at his country home, Gad's Hill Place, in Rochester, Kent.

Designed to look like a bookcase, its shelves displayed fake titles such as *The Life of a Cat, in Nine Volumes* and *The History of a Short Chancery Suit, in 47 Volumes.*

The latter was a reference to the very long Chancery case that inspired his novel *Bleak House.*

"Have a heart that never hardens,
and a temper that never tires, and
a touch that never hurts."

Hard Times, 1854

"There is a wisdom of the head, and … there is a wisdom of the heart.**"**

Hard Times, 1854

"There is prodigious strength in sorrow and despair."

A Tale of Two Cities, 1859

"My advice is, never do to-morrow what you can do today. Procrastination is the thief of time. Collar him!"

David Copperfield, 1850

Dickens' final novel, *The Mystery of Edwin Drood*, has remained a mystery. On 8 June 1870, Dickens had been working on the book at his country home when he suffered a stroke.

He died the following day – at the age of 58 – leaving the question of what happened to the main character unsolved. In 2015, however, a University of Buckingham project called *The Drood Inquiry* concluded that Drood had been murdered by his uncle.

"Look round and round upon this bare bleak plain, and see even here, upon a winter's day, how beautiful the shadows are! Alas! it is the nature of their kind to be so. The loveliest things in life, Tom, are but shadows; and they come and go, and change and fade away, as rapidly as these!"

Martin Chuzzlewit, 1844

"Are not the sane and the insane equal at night as the sane lie a dreaming? Are not all of us outside this hospital, who dream, more or less in the condition of those inside it, every night of our lives?... I wonder that the great master who knew everything, when he called Sleep the death of each day's life, did not call Dreams the insanity of each day's sanity."

The Uncommercial Traveller – Night Walks, 1860–61

"Heaven knows we need never be ashamed of our tears, for they are rain upon the blinding dust of earth, overlying our hard hearts."

Great Expectations, 1861

"In the moonlight which is always sad, as the light of the sun itself is — as the light called human life is — at its coming and its going."

A Tale of Two Cities, 1859

Although he was a worldwide celebrity, Dickens wanted to be buried quietly at Rochester Cathedral, in Kent.

Despite his wishes, however, he was interred in the Poets' Corner of Westminster Abbey, in the company of literary greats such as Geoffrey Chaucer, John Dryden and Samuel Johnson.

"He had a large loving mind and the strongest sympathy with the poorer classes. He felt sure a better feeling, and much greater union of classes, would take place in time. And I pray earnestly it may."

Queen Victoria, in a diary entry, 11 June 1870

"**V**ices are sometimes only virtues carried to excess!"

Dombey and Son, 1848

"From the death of each day's hope another hope sprung up to live to-morrow."

The Old Curiosity Shop, 1841

"Happiness is a gift and the trick is not to expect it, but to delight in it when it comes."

Nicholas Nickleby, 1839

Illustration by Fred Barnard, from an 1875 edition of *Nicholas Nickleby*

"A loving heart is the truest wisdom."

David Copperfield, 1850